To : Austin ("fo   s

2-23-01

Love Grandma & Grandpa K.

D𝒾sney's

American Frontier #1

DAVY CROCKETT
AND THE KING OF THE RIVER
Based on the Walt Disney Television Show

Written by A. L. Singer
Cover Illustrated by Mike Wepplo
Illustrated by Charlie Shaw

D𝒾sney
PRESS
NEW YORK

FIRST EDITION
1   3   5   7   9   10   8   6   4   2

Library of Congress Catalog Card Number: 91-71356
ISBN 1-56282-007-9/1-56282-006-0 (lib. bdg.)

Consultant: Judith A. Brundin, Supervisory Education Specialist
National Museum of the American Indian
Smithsonian Institution, New York

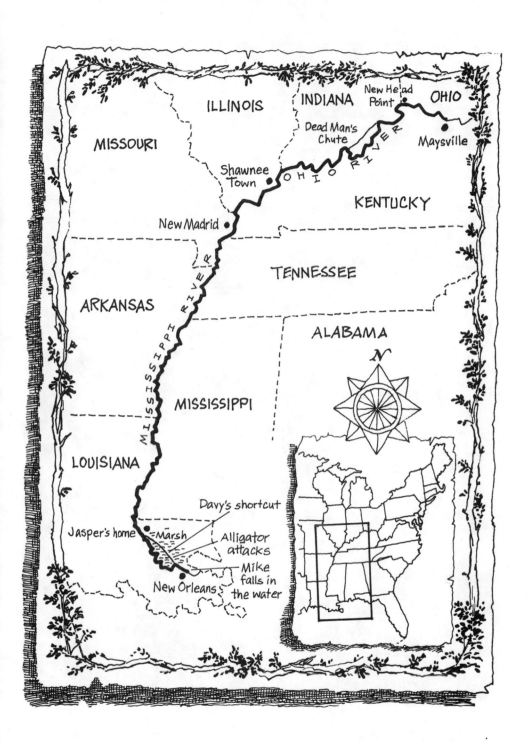

CHAPTER 1

"Yee-ouch! These Kentucky ants got a bite like an alligator!" Georgie Russel shouted. He jumped away from the campfire and began scratching his ankles. "It's bad enough we been walking and walking *and walking* for weeks. Now these little critters won't even let us settle down!"

Davy Crockett chuckled. "Georgie, if you ain't bragging about something, you're complaining." Using a sturdy twig, Davy poked the fire. Aside from the full moon, its glowing red coals were the only light in the dark forest.

Foosh! Suddenly flames shot upward. They danced around the pot of coffee and a pan of beef stew.

"Well, I think I got a reason to complain, Davy." Georgie sat down by the fire and held up one foot. There was a large hole in the bottom of his moccasin. "Look at that, would you? All worn out. My dang feet will be next! We ain't never been on a hunt that lasted this long."

"Yep," Davy said. "We ain't never got so many fur pelts before, either, Georgie." Smiling broadly, he admired the pile of animal skins lying on the ground next to their horses.

Davy had big plans for those skins. He'd heard he could get a good price for them way down south in the town of Natchez, Mississippi. But Natchez was hundreds of miles away. To get there, they would have to ride down the Ohio River, which flowed into the Mississippi River. The Mississippi River ran all the way to Louisiana.

"How much longer you figure we gotta walk, anyhow?" Georgie wanted to know.

"Well, if I figured it right, we ought to reach a place called Maysville before noon tomorrow," Davy replied. "The Ohio River flows right through the center of town."

"Well," Georgie said, pouring himself some coffee, "the pack horses are plumb worn out from the load, and so am I. I sure hope we can hitch a boat ride there."

"Me too," Davy agreed. "We ought to make some good money for our pelts down in Natchez."

Georgie stretched out on the ground. "You ain't fooling me none. You ain't thinking about the price of furs. You're thinking about all that new country we're going to be looking at."

"Guess you're right, Georgie," Davy said. If there was one thing Davy Crockett loved, it was a new adventure. In fact, Davy had had so many adventures that they had become legendary stories told by people far and wide. Some said he could wrestle a wild animal with his bare hands. Some said he could track with the best of the Indians. Others claimed he had caught a bear when he was only three years old.

"I've been a lot of places and done a lot of things," Davy said, "but I've never been on a river ride this long."

Georgie let out a long yawn. "Just thinking about it makes me tired. I think I'm going to turn in for the night."

" 'Night, Georgie," Davy said.

" 'Night," Georgie said .

Davy sipped his coffee and stared into the campfire. Crazy thoughts tumbled around in his head about the river adventure to come. There would be wild water currents, strange new sights along the shores, and maybe animals he had never seen before. Davy couldn't wait. He felt ready for whatever tough challenge lay ahead.

CHAPTER 2

The next day Davy and Georgie arrived at the sleepy town of Maysville, Kentucky. In their dirty, rumpled clothes, Davy and Georgie looked like two scraggly peddlers pulling their horses. Townspeople had no idea they were passing the legendary Davy Crockett.

In no time Davy and Georgie found just what they were looking for: the Ohio River, flowing right through the middle of town. A boat was pulling in to the dock. It was a keelboat, with a wide long deck and a flat bottom. The deck floated inches above the water. Its crew moved the boat by pushing against the shallow river bottom with long poles.

"Here comes our boat ride," Davy said. "Let's hitch up."

As they tied up their horses, they could hear the boat's crew singing at the top of their lungs. "Listen to the thunder, hear the wind roar, hurricane's a coming,

board up the door! Girls run and hide, brave men shiver! He's Mike Fink, King of the River!"

"What are they singing so loud about?" Georgie asked.

Davy shrugged. "Something's sure got their fur riled up."

As they walked closer to the boat, two big men stepped off. The first one had legs like tree trunks, arms to match, and a scowl that could curdle milk. But it was the second man that Davy noticed most.

The second man made the first one seem puny. His shoulders were like small mountains. His hands were the size of a pair of bear cubs, and just as hairy. His beady eyes glared out from underneath a tall, green felt hat with a single bright red feather in its band. In his right hand he clutched a thick rope as easily as if it were a skinny thread. With a flick of his wrist, he snapped the rope. Quick as a wink, it whipped around the wooden dock pole and held fast.

"That ought to keep her from drifting," he said. His voice was somewhere between a foghorn and a dog's bark.

"Excuse me, Mister, can you tell me which one of them fellers is the Captain?" Davy asked, pointing toward the boat.

The man with the feathered hat turned slowly to face him. He was so tall, Davy found himself looking at the huge man's Adam's apple.

"What did you say?" the man asked with a sneer.

The other man laughed. "He wants to know who the Captain is!"

"How long you bushwhackers been holed up in the backwoods?" the man with the hat said. *Everybody* knows the Captain of the *Gullywhumper*. It's me, Mike Fink, King of the River!"

Georgie stepped in front of Davy. "Well, Captain, meet up with Davy Crockett, King of the Wild Frontier!"

Mike Fink narrowed his eyes. "Davy Crockett, eh? Well, it sure is a small world. You're about a foot shorter than you ought to be."

"Don't worry," Georgie told him. "He's still growing!"

"Yeah," Mike growled, "like them stories they keep spreading about you."

Davy nodded. "Mighty hard to live up to."

"Well, I don't have no trouble living up to stories about me!" Mike bellowed. "I am the original ring-tailed roarer from the thunder-and-lightning country. I'm a real snorter and a head buster. I can outrun, outjump, outsing, outswim, outdance, outshoot, outeat—"

"Out*talk*?" Davy interrupted.

"Yeah, I can outtalk and outfight anybody on the whole Mississippi and Ohio rivers put together!" Mike yelled.

Davy tried not to look as bored with all this boasting

as he felt. "Mighty interesting," he said, "but all we want to know is how far down the river are you going?"

"Why, all the way to New Orleans, of course!" Mike said. "I told you I'm Mike Fink, King of the River. This is my own private river."

"Well, have you got room for a couple of passengers?" Georgie asked.

"Where you headed?" Mike asked.

"Natchez," Davy answered. "We got some furs we aim to sell down there."

Mike looked over at the furs piled on the pack horses. "Well, you can get a better price for your furs in New Orleans," he said with a raised eyebrow. "Tell you what I'll do, seeing as it's you. I'll give you a special rate."

Davy smiled. "Well, that's mighty nice of you."

"Yes," Mike said. "Uh . . . you and your furs all the way to Natchez, or New Orleans . . ." He scrunched up his brow, figuring out the price.

Davy looked at Georgie and winked, as if to say, "See, he's not so bad, after all."

But he changed his mind when he heard Mike's next words. "For you, only a thousand dollars, cash up front."

Davy's jaw dropped. Big Mike Fink wasn't just a braggart. He was a crook, too!

CHAPTER 3

"**A** thousand dollars?" Georgie shouted. "You know we ain't got that kind of money. You're nothing but a low-down thief!"

"Ain't no question about it," Mike said. "Make up your minds, and let me know before morning."

With that, he and his partner walked away.

"Who does that big windbag think he is?" Georgie mumbled.

"Seems like he told us," Davy said. "The King of the River."

As Georgie watched Mike strut up the street, he caught a glimpse of another keelboat. It was docked near a boating supply shop, and its deck was loaded with barrels marked New Orleans. In front of the boat a grizzled old man was hammering a nail into its hull.

"Well, Mike Fink might be the King of the River," Georgie replied, pointing, "but he ain't got the only boat! Look over there!"

Davy grinned. "Let's go talk to the Captain," he said.

Georgie called out, "Howdy!"

The old man looked up. Davy could tell from his face that he was a river man. His skin was tan from years of too much sun, and the deep creases around his eyes told of years of staring upriver while the bright sun glinted off the water.

"This your boat?" Georgie asked.

"Yep," the old man answered. "She's called the *Bertha Mae*."

"Looks like a fast one," Davy said.

The old man answered, "Purty hard to beat, if she's handled right."

"Which way are you going?" Davy asked. "Upriver or down?"

"Ain't going no place right now," the man said.

"Your barrels are marked for New Orleans," said Georgie.

The old man nodded. "That's right, but I'm blamed if I know how they're getting there. I can't get a crew together."

"Why not?" Davy asked.

"They heard about the Indians," the man said.

"Indians?" Davy said, surprised. "Why, I know the tribes around here, Mister. They're among the most peace-lovin' folk I ever met—"

"Tain't here," the man said. "It's downriver somewhere, t'other side of Shawneetown. Indians are attacking everything—flatboats loaded with settlers, even armed keelboats. It's got so bad, nobody'd sign on to my boat."

Davy shook his head. "Don't sound right to me. Somebody must have done something purty awful to those Indians to get them so angry. And even so, they wouldn't attack innocent people."

The man shrugged. "All's I know is what I hear. Plenty of people been hurt."

"Doesn't seem to be scaring off Mike Fink none," Georgie said.

The old man wrinkled his face into a sour expression. "Ah, him and them thieving pole pushers of his ain't human enough to be scared!"

Georgie sighed. "Looks like we picked the wrong time for a boat ride."

As he and Davy turned to leave, the old man suddenly said, "Hey, are you really Davy Crockett?"

"Why, sure," Davy answered.

For the first time, the old man rose to his feet. A tiny smile flickered across his face as he stuck out his hand. "I'm Captain Cobb."

Davy shook his hand. "This here's my friend, Georgie Russel."

"Glad to know ya," Cobb said.

"Howdy," Georgie replied.

"You fellers got quite a reputation when it comes to making friends with the Indians," Cobb said. "Now, if folks knew you were going downriver with me, maybe we could get ourselves a crew."

Davy nodded. "What do you think, Georgie?" he asked.

"Beats paying a thousand dollars that we ain't got," Georgie answered.

Davy turned to Cobb. "How many men would it take?"

"Six all together," Cobb replied, "if they're all as sturdy as you two."

"Well, maybe you'll need more," Davy said. "Georgie and I don't know much about boating."

"All's I need is men who can learn," Cobb said. "If you can find 'em, you got your boat ride."

"You've got yourself a deal, Captain," Davy said. "We'll see you back here before sundown."

Davy and Georgie made arrangements to board their horses at a nearby stable. Then they walked into town.

Maysville was a much bigger place than Davy had thought at first. The sun was shining brightly, and the streets were full. People hustled around, laughing, arguing, eating, strolling. Someone was filling a trough full of water for horses to drink during the hot afternoon.

"We'd better split if we're going to cover the town," Davy said.

"Now don't be afraid to tell people who you are,"

Georgie said. "Toot your own horn a little. Remember, we *need* to find a crew."

"Well *you* mind your bragging," Davy warned. "Don't be making promises we can't keep."

Georgie looked wounded. "Aw, now, you know me, Davy."

"I sure do," Davy replied, "and I know you don't mean to do it, but your tongue wagging's got us into hot water before and—"

They both turned at the sound of angry shouts. "Hey! Hey, you!" a small red-faced man called out, shaking his fist. Just ahead of him, an enormous man was carrying a huge barrel toward a restaurant. The barrel must have weighed as much as a grizzly bear, Davy thought. It was certainly big enough, but the man wasn't straining at all. He just puffed happily on a fat cigar.

"Hey, what's the idea of blowing that cigar in my face?" the small man demanded.

The man with the barrel turned slowly. Without saying a word, he blew a puff of smoke right in the small man's face.

"Hrrrum—pkaachhh!" the man coughed, and backed away. The water trough was now a few feet behind him.

The man with the cigar calmly put the barrel down, stepped toward the other man, and blew another puff.

Then he rolled up his sleeves and gave him a good, hard push.

"Whoooooa!" With a loud splash, the small man fell backward into the trough.

There were a few gasps and giggles among the people in the street. The man with the cigar gave a snort of triumph, hoisted the barrel to his shoulders, and walked away.

"What a bully," Davy muttered.

Georgie smiled. "Yeah, and he's just about the right size for our boat!" he thought. He took off after the man, calling to Davy over his shoulder, "See you back at the landing!"

The man disappeared through the swinging doors of a restaurant. Georgie hurried to follow him. He heard shouting and then smashing. Suddenly the restaurant door crashed open and a man came flying through and landed in a heap. He scrambled to his feet and looked back to the building. There, standing in the doorway with an evil grin, was the man with the cigar.

"Now, anybody else in this town don't care for my cigar?" he rasped.

Georgie walked right up to him and said, "Kind of handy with those fists of yours, ain't you?"

"Ah, I'm better at kicking and biting," the man growled.

"You're just the kind of feller I've been looking for," Georgie said. "Can I buy you lunch?"

The man's face twisted into a gap-toothed smile. "Hey, you're just the kind of feller I've been looking for, too."

Georgie reached up and clapped the man's shoulder. It was like holding onto a rock. Together they walked into the restaurant.

"Can I asked what was in that barrel?" Georgie said.

"Sugar," the man told him. "I guess you can say I'm a salesman."

"Get a good price?"

The man grinned. "I get whatever price I want." Then he shouted across the room to a waiter, "Four steaks! Make 'em rare and make 'em fast!"

"Four?" Georgie asked. "You expecting company?"

"Three for me and one for you," the man answered.

"You want to know something?" Georgie said. "A sleepy little old river town like this ain't no place for a man of your talents."

The man nodded. "Mister, that's a fact."

"What's your name?"

"Jocko."

"Mine's Georgie."

"Well, I'm pleased to meet you."

"Hey, Jocko, how'd you like to see a little something of the world?"

Jocko narrowed his eyes. "What are you driving at, Georgie?"

"I'll let you in on something," Georgie said, leaning

over the table. "Me and *Davy Crockett* are getting a little party to take a boat ride down the river."

"Take a *what?*" Jocko barked.

"Boat ride!" Georgie said. "On the *Bertha Mae.* Clean down to New Orleans."

Jocko grinned, then chuckled, then burst into deep laughter.

"What's so funny?" Georgie asked.

"Oh, that's the gall-bustingest joke I ever heard!" Jocko said. He turned and yelled across the room. "Hey, Mike! This clodhopper's trying to sign old Jocko on the *Bertha Mae!*"

Mike?

Georgie felt his blood run cold. He turned slowly around to see who Jocko was talking to.

Looming over Georgie, his arms crossed, was Mike Fink. "You tired of living?" he said through clenched teeth. "Nobody tries to steal one of Mike Fink's crew!"

CHAPTER 4

Well, how'd I know this . . . this little hyena . . . this little squirt . . . was one of your hyenas?" Georgie stammered.

"I accept your apology," Mike said, pulling up a chair. "Couple more steaks!" he shouted over his shoulder to a waiter.

"At this rate, we should have ordered a whole cow in advance," Georgie remarked.

"A whole cow! That's a good one!" Mike bellowed, slapping his knee. Then he turned serious. "Now tell me something. Ain't you heard about them Indians downriver?"

"Yeah, but Indians don't scare Davy none," Georgie bragged. "Soon as we get a crew together we'll be on our way."

"Well, you ain't going to find no keelboat crew around here. And if any of these cornhuskers are crazy enough to join up with you, you'll end up in a sandbar for sure!" Mike shook his head. "I just can't understand how a couple of smart fellers like you and Davy Crockett could turn me down for a bumbling old coot like Cap Cobb."

"Cobb's a good man," Georgie said with a shrug, "and a fair one. *He* ain't charging us a thousand dollars."

"Well, it's your funeral," Mike answered.

Just then a waiter staggered over to the table with a tray full of fat, juicy steaks. "I want three of your biggest for old Georgie here," Mike said, "And that'll be just to get his appetite going."

"Three?" Georgie said. "How am I going to—"

"What are you, a man or a mouse?" Mike taunted. "Don't tell me you ain't got room for a few steaks."

"I'm eating four," Jocko said. "Usually I eat six but I'm trying to lose weight."

Georgie tried to hold his tongue. Davy's words echoed in his mind: *"You mind your bragging, Georgie!"* He wasn't going to let Davy down.

Mike cackled, then said to the waiter, "old Georgie here ain't man enough to eat a real meal. Just bring him a piece of toast."

"Who ain't man enough?" Georgie sputtered. Mike and Jocko were laughing at him. So were a couple of people at the next table. Even the waiter was snickering.

Georgie felt the blood rush to his face. He could hold his tongue no longer. "Course I'm man enough!" he explained. "You ask my friend, Davy. He says nobody has a bigger appetite this side of the Mississippi. Why, I can outeat *anybody*!"

"Well, that's right nice," Mike replied. " 'Cause if you're going to be a river man, you got to learn to eat like one!"

"Ha! I'll show you!" Georgie's eyes flashed and he puffed out his chest. By now he had completely forgotten his promise to Davy. "A river man! I could outpole you on a keelboat with my eyes closed. Waiter, give me those steaks!"

The waiter plopped three plates in front of Georgie. Each held one of the most enormous steaks he had ever seen. Each one could have been an animal all by itself.

On either side of him, Jocko and Mike stared. "Well, what are you waiting for?" Mike said. "As long as you're paying for 'em, Georgie boy, you may as well enjoy 'em!"

"Long as I'm *what?*" Georgie said. "I can't—"

"You wouldn't want it to get around town that Georgie Russel skipped out on his bill," Mike said. "Or that you couldn't eat as much as old Jocko here."

" 'Course I can," Georgie said defiantly.

The waiter put four plates in front of Jocko. "Prove it," Mike said, as Jocko rolled up his sleeves. "And waiter, bring us a couple more for good measure."

Georgie took a deep gulp. Well, he *was* pretty hungry. Under the watchful eyes of Mike and Jocko, he picked up his knife and fork and dug in.

At the back of a warehouse a few streets away, Davy Crockett met two strapping young men. One was blond and the other had black hair. "Hey, fellers," Davy called out. "You work here full-time?"

"Nope," the blond fellow answered. "Why?"

"How'd you like to help crew the *Bertha Mae* down the Ohio?" Davy asked.

"The *who?*" the black-haired man asked.

"Mighty exciting adventures in store for whoever wants to take a chance," Davy said.

"Say," the blond man said, squinting at Davy's face, "ain't you Davy Crockett?"

"That's what they tell me," Davy answered.

Both men broke into wide smiles. "Well, you can count me in!" the blond one said, shaking Davy's hand. "Name's Ben Manvell!"

"And I'm Hank Hall," the black-haired man said.

"Welcome aboard," Davy said. "Now all's we need is four more men. Come on and I'll introduce you to Georgie Russel. He's around here somewhere."

But Georgie wasn't in the street, or in the restaurant. In fact, he wasn't in the General Store, the post office, or the bakery.

Finally Hank said, "You keep looking for him, Davy. We'll find the rest of the fellers you need."

"Yeah," Ben said. "Might take a little persuading, but we'll have a full crew on the landing before morning."

"Mighty obliging of you fellers," Davy said.

Hank smiled. "Well, anything for you, Davy."

The two men hurried off, leaving Davy on the street. Suddenly he heard a strange, low moan.

"Mooohhh. . . ," the sound went.

Davy turned to see Mike and Jocko coming around the side of the restaurant, holding Georgie up in between them.

"Georgie?" Davy said.

"Mooohhhh. . . ," Georgie repeated.

Mike and Jocko were all smiles. "He had a bit too much to eat," Mike explained. "Guess he wasn't used to the size of them steaks they serve in these parts."

"Not to mention the mashed potatoes and corn and biscuits," Jocko said.

George moaned again. All this talk of food was making his face slowly turn green.

"I think it was the three hot-fudge sundaes that did him in," Mike said.

"Mmmmmph!" George blurted. At the mention of dessert, his eyes grew wide and his hands shot up to cover his mouth. He stumbled toward the back of the restaurant as fast as his shaky legs could carry him.

"Georgie!" Davy called after him.

"Goldarn, did I say the wrong thing?" Mike asked innocently.

"Must have a weak stomach," Jocko said. "Har, har, har, har!"

Mike put his right hand on Davy's shoulder. "Ah, don't worry, Crockett. Your buddy lost this bet, but you both got a chance to beat us on the next one."

Davy looked at him blankly. "What are you jabbering about? Beat you on what?"

"Why, the race, of course," Mike said.

"Race?" Davy repeated. "What kind of race?"

"Keelboats! What else?" Mike replied. "The *Gullywhumper* against the *Bertha Mae* to New Orleans, Louisiana."

Davy's eyes opened wide. He couldn't believe what he was hearing. "We can't race you!"

Mike shrugged his enormous shoulders. "Well, that's what I told Georgie, but he wouldn't believe me. He insisted on betting that you could win!"

"What?" Davy said.

"That's right," Mike replied. "Seems old Georgie ordered this big meal, then couldn't pay for it. Well, the waiter got mighty angry, so I put the money up myself. That's when Georgie struck up a little wager." Mike grinned. "The terms are simple. If we win, we get your furs, and Georgie pays me double the money for the steaks. If you win, your friend doesn't have to pay, and you get to be called King of the River!"

"Georgie knows better than that!" Davy protested. "Why, it took us all winter to get them furs."

Mike just grinned and folded his arms. With a wink to Jocko, he said, "Ain't that too bad. Oh, well, my crew is gonna look mighty fancy in coonskin caps."

As Georgie staggered back around the restaurant, Mike and Jocko exploded with laughter.

CHAPTER 5

"I don't know, Davy, I guess, I guess we just got to talking," Georgie said, trying to keep up with Davy. They were heading down the main street.

"Talking?" Davy said angrily. "You mean *bragging*, just like I warned you not to."

"I'm awful sorry, Davy. Awful sorry."

"Being sorry isn't going to get us to New Orleans ahead of Mike Fink."

"Well, couldn't you just tell him I was only fooling?"

Davy stopped and looked his friend squarely in the eyes. "You really think he'd let you off that easy?"

"Oh, I reckon not," Georgie said, with a sigh. "I'll never do it again, Davy."

Davy turned to walk again. "You bet you won't. I'm sure not willing to let another winter's worth of hunting go toward a dinner you couldn't even eat!"

"I know, I know," Georgie said, clutching his stomach. "Now we *really* got to find ourselves a crew."

"Not in your condition," Davy told him grimly. "You get back to the boat and have Cap Cobb put you to bed while I gather up the gear."

Georgie's face brightened. "Thank you, Davy. You're mighty understanding."

Davy watched Georgie hobble off. He shook his head, then went into the General Store.

"Pardon me, sir," Davy said to the old man behind the counter. "You know of any big, strong fellers might take a shine to a long boat ride down the Ohio?"

The man chuckled. "Must be a lot of boats leaving. Somebody else come in here not five minutes ago asking the same thing. Matter of fact, there he goes now."

Davy looked outside to see Hank crossing the street. "Much obliged," he said, and left to catch up with Hank.

"Did you find your partner yet?" Hank asked.

"Sure did," Davy answered.

"Good," Hank said. "Ben got us a feller named Leif. The two of them are over on the next street talking to some other fellers that've got a hankering to see New Orleans."

Davy felt some of his bad mood begin to lift. "Let's see how they made out," he said.

He followed Hank through a back alley into a lot

behind a row of buildings. There were piles of lumber around, but no people.

"That's funny," Hank said. "They was here a minute ago."

Crrrrasshh!

Suddenly a stack of two-by-fours clattered to the ground. Behind it, heads bobbed up and down and fists flew. Six men tumbled about, all fighting so hard and fast, it was impossible to tell who was who.

"There they are," said Hank.

"I thought you said they was *talking*," Davy said. He ran around the pile of wood, shouting, "Hey, fellers, take it easy! We don't want anybody that ain't willing!"

Ben rose out the pile of bodies and said, "They *are* willing, Davy." He pointed to a man on the ground, wrapped up in a horse blanket and struggling to get out. "This feller's accusing us of stealing men from *his* trip! He's the one started the fight."

Davy leaned over the man on the ground and pulled the blanket off him. The man spun around, swinging his arms wildly, grunting with the strain.

Davy shook his head. "Can't leave you alone for a minute, can I, Georgie?"

Georgie froze. Slowly his face turned red, and a sheepish smile came across his face. "Uh, sorry, Davy," he said. "I thought . . . I thought . . . ohhhh, does my stomach hurt!"

CHAPTER 6

Early the next morning, the Maysville dock was bursting with activity. News of the race between the *Gully-whumper* and the *Bertha Mae*—that is, the race between Mike Fink and Davy Crockett—had spread through the town like wildfire. A crowd had gathered to see the start of the race. A grandstand had been hastily erected for the town's officials to preside over the event.

"I say Davy Crockett by three miles!" a teenager shouted.

"Big Mike'll be there and back before Crockett makes it to Louisiana!" yelled someone else.

In the shallow water of the Ohio River, the two crews manned their poles. They plunged their poles into the river bottom, then pushed hard. Slowly the boats floated to the starting position, even with an orange flag near the grandstand.

Davy held his pole fast. The *Bertha Mae* was ready. He looked at the crowd and felt his blood quicken with

excitement. He caught a glimpse of Georgie, grinning and holding on to his pole. But next to Georgie, Davy saw Ben struggling with *his* pole. It seemed to be stuck. Captain Cobb, positioned at the tiller, saw him, too. Cobb called out, "You okay, Manvell?"

"Aye-aye, sir. I mean no-aye, sir," Ben answered. "I mean it's *stuck*!"

Ben tried to pull his pole free, but it pulled him instead. He plunged over the side, and belly flopped into the river with a huge splash.

The pole swayed slightly in the breeze, but remained upright. There was a roar from the *Gullywhumper*, and from the crowd. Davy turned his head. Captain Cobb rolled his eyes.

"Citizens of Maysville!" the town magistrate shouted from the grandstand. "You are about to witness the start of a historical event. This will be remembered as the classic contest of all time! A keelboat race between the intrepid Davy Crockett of Tennessee—" A loud cheer rose up from the crowd.

"—and the undefeated Mike Fink, King of the River!" The magistrate turned to the two keelboats. "Are the Captains ready?"

From the deck of the *Gullywhumper*, Mike shouted, "I'm ready!"

Captain Cobb watched two men fish Ben out of the water. He sighed and turned to the magistrate. "I guess I'm as ready as I'll ever be."

"Hey, Crockett!" Mike yelled. "Might as well give me them furs right now!"

"You ain't won 'em yet!" Davy called back.

With a cocky smile, Mike took off his felt hat and waved it. "Well, if I don't win 'em. I'll eat my hat, red feather and all!"

"Now, *that's* something I'd like to see," Davy replied. "You got a deal, partner!"

A burst of laughter bellowed across the river. The *Gullywhumper* crewmen seemed to think that was the funniest thing they'd ever heard. They slapped their knees, pointed mockingly at the *Bertha Mae*, and pretended to eat their own hats.

Georgie sidled up beside Davy. "One of these days," he muttered, "that big blowhard's going to get what's coming to him."

The magistrate's voice cut through the laughter. "Take your starting positions!" he barked.

Mike grabbed the tiller of the *Gullywhumper*. Cobb grabbed the tiller of the *Bertha Mae*.

"Stand by!" Mike called to his crew.

"Stand by!" Cobb called to his.

The men on the deck of the *Bertha Mae* flew into total confusion. Some went left, some right. Poles collided. Cobb buried his face in his hands and moaned, "No, no, no! Jumping catfish, do it the way I told you!"

On the *Gullywhumper*, Mike and his men were practically doubled over with laughter.

"Now remember," the magistrate called out, "no one starts until the cannon fires." With a grand sweep of his hand, he lit a match and held it to the fuse.

"Get ready!" Mike commanded his crew.

"Get ready, boys!" Cobb pleaded.

Booooom!

They were off. Davy, Georgie, Ben, Hank, Leif, and the others thrust their poles into the river. When they hit bottom, they pushed with all their might. The *Bertha Mae* jerked forward.

"That's right, fellers!" Cobb shouted.

But the *Gullywhumper* was already pulling ahead. At the tiller, Mike began singing the same song Davy and Georgie had heard the day before: "Listen to the thunder, hear the wind roar. . . ."

"He isn't half bad," Georgie told Davy.

" 'Course not," Davy replied. "He's singing about his favorite topic—himself!"

Soon the entire *Gullywhumper* crew joined in for the chorus:

"Oh, he's a ring-tailed roarer
And a tough old lizard.
Oh, his arms are like steel
And his heart is like a gizzard.
Oh, what a fighting devil,
He'll spit in your eye.
He's going to live forever,
Born too tough to die!"

The *Gullywhumper* was speeding ahead now. Davy and Georgie dug in as hard as they could. Around them, the others were huffing and puffing. "It ain't no use, Davy!" Georgie said, panting, "We ain't going to catch them."

"Hey, where's your fighting spirit?" Davy answered. "We just got started. What we need is a song like they've got."

"Yeah! Let's sing one!" Georgie said.

"Got any ideas?" Davy asked.

"*Me?*" Georgie said.

"You've got the biggest mouth," Davy replied with a grin. "Besides, you made up some pretty good songs while we was hunting."

Georgie dug his pole in and thought hard. "Okay," he said. "I'm getting an idea. Just let me figure out the rhymes."

It took him a few moments, but the song came out loud and clear:

"He don't take nothing from no man at all,
The bigger they brag, the harder they fall.
The tougher they are, the louder they squall.
When they get what-for in a free-for-all!
Davy, Davy Crockett, King of the Wild Frontier!"

One by one, the other men joined in, and before long their song rang out across the river:

"Ain't no trick at all to poling keelboats;
We can beat Mike Fink with anything that floats!

We've got the hang, we're feeling our oats;
We'll shove their brags right down their ornery
throats!
Davy, Davy Crockett, King of the Wild Frontier!"

Sure enough, while they sang, the *Bertha Mae*
picked up speed. The *Gullywhumper* was still ahead, but
they were catching up. Maysville disappeared from sight
behind them, and the Ohio wound its way through farm-
land and forests.

On the *Gullywhumper*, Mike sprawled lazily in a
chair, guiding the tiller with his feet. "Look at them
clodhoppers, would you?" he said.

Jocko's eyes *were* fixed on the *Bertha Mae*, but he
looked worried. He began pacing back and forth. Suddenly he tripped over something large and soft.

He looked down to see a crewmate fast asleep. Jocko
yelled, "Wake up, Moose!" Moose's eyes blinked. "Huh?
Was I snoring again?"

"On your feet!" Jocko snapped. "They're catching
up!"

The *Gullywhumper* was about to go around a bend.
With a yawn, Mike stood up. "Don't strain yourselves,
boys. They ain't going to catch us."

Mike knew that a band of Indians were hidden in
the bushes just before the bend. He'd seen them many
times before on trips downriver. And he knew that if left
alone, the Indians would not try to attack. But, if pro-
voked, they would surely be ready to defend themselves.

Mike picked up a shotgun, aimed it high in the air over by the Indians, waited a few seconds, and then fired, just as the *Gullywhumper* slipped around the bend, out of the Indians' sight.

Craccckkk!

The Indians sprang to their feet when they heard the gunshot. But they could see only one keelboat—the *Bertha Mae*!

On board the *Bertha Mae*, Captain Cobb looked puzzled. "Them's the Miami tribe," he said. "What did Mike Fink want to shoot at them for? They's friendly."

Zhiing! An arrow whizzed right by his ear.

Zhiing! Another one lodged in the deck, inches from Georgie's feet.

"You mean they *was* friendly!" Georgie said with a gulp.

CHAPTER 7

hiing! Zhiing! Zhiing! Zhiing!

A storm of arrows flew around them. Davy and Georgie ducked. The entire *Bertha Mae* crew fell to the deck and hid behind the cabin.

"Hey!" Captain Cobb shouted to the Indians. "We ain't the ones that shot at you!"

The Indians kept shooting. With the crew all in hiding now, the *Bertha Mae* was a sitting target. Something had to be done. Davy quickly got up and began poling.

"That's it, Davy!" Georgie shouted. He grabbed his pole, too. "Come on, fellers, man your poles and let's get out of here!"

The crew began to pole furiously. The *Bertha Mae* picked up speed as it rounded the bend in the river.

"That's the dirtiest trick I ever saw," Davy yelled angrily. "Starting up trouble with a friendly Indian tribe, making them waste all their arrows—"

"Well, I'm just glad they didn't waste 'em between

my ears," Georgie replied. "That rotten Mike Fink could have gotten us killed!"

Davy's jaw was set with determination. "Don't worry," he said. "We'll pay him back. For us and the Miami. Any place up ahead he'll come in close to shore?"

"Yep," Cobb replied. "He'll be rounding New Head Point sometime tonight. After that there's a channel that runs close along the Indiana shore for miles."

"How much rope you got aboard?" Davy asked.

"Oh, two or three hundred feet," Cobb answered. "Why?"

Davy was deep in thought. He had a plan that would teach old Mike Fink a lesson. "I'm thinking I'll have you put me ashore as soon as it's dark," he said.

It was pitch-dark when the *Bertha Mae* approached New Head Point. At the prow Davy strained his eyes, trying to make out shapes on the shore. "We getting there yet, Cobb?" he asked.

Cobb looked at his compass. " 'Nother quarter mile or so," he said.

"How 'bout the *Gullywhumper*?"

"Can't see them, so I reckon they're around the bend already."

"Just what I wanted to hear," Davy said. "Pull her over near the shore."

"Whatever you say, Davy," Cobb turned around and called out to his crew, "All right, let's take her hard to port, men!"

"Ssssh!" Davy warned. "We want to get as close to them as we can without being noticed."

Georgie, Ben, and Leif poled the *Bertha Mae* close to an old rickety landing by the riverbank. With Captain Cobb's rope coiled around his shoulders, Davy stepped onto the landing and waved good-bye to the crew.

New Head Point was a thin strip of land covered with pine trees that jutted into the water. It took longer for a boat on the river to sail around the point than it did for a man on land to cross it by foot. By running straight across the point, Davy got ahead of the *Gullywhumper*.

He crouched down in the darkness and waited. Sure enough, he soon heard a soft splashing sound. There was the *Gullywhumper*, barging through the water.

Davy quickly climbed up a thick, sturdy tree. He tied a large loop in the rope and waited silently for the *Gullywhumper* to pass by him.

As it got closer, he could see Mike on deck, fast asleep with a smile on his face.

In the rear of the boat was the anchor reel. Davy lowered the the looped end of the rope, and carefully guided it toward the reel. The rope looped around it, then slipped off.

Davy tried again. This time it worked. Davy had lassoed the *Gullywhumper*. He tugged gently until the loop held fast.

He let out the rest of the rope, giving the *Gully-whumper* lots of slack. He figured it would take about

five minutes for the *Gullywhumper* to pull the entire rope tight. That would be just enough time for Davy—and the other end of the rope—to get back to the *Bertha Mae.*

He scrambled down from the tree just as the *Bertha Mae* came around the bend. Davy ran along shore to meet it. Then he waded in the shallow water.

"Grab ahold, Davy!" Georgie said, leaning over the side.

Davy took his hand and climbed aboard. He let the coiled rope drop to the deck. As it started to unravel, he tied the end of it to the railing of the *Bertha Mae.*

Within seconds the rope pulled tight. The *Bertha Mae* lurched forward. It was being pulled by the *Gullywhumper.*

"Well, Georgie," Davy said, "looks like we can sit down and get some rest now."

"Put your feet up, boys!" Georgie shouted.

On the *Gullywhumper*, Mike was now awake, but he barely noticed when his boat made a sudden little jerk.

"Hey, what happened?" came a gruff shout from one of Mike's men.

"Must have hit a sandbar," Mike answered.

Beside him, Jocko turned around and stared upriver. "Hey! Hey, Mike!" he yelled, poking Mike in the shoulder. "Look!"

Mike threw a quick glance backward. The *Bertha Mae* was following behind at the same speed as the *Gully-*

whumper. He could make out the crew members sitting on deck. "Oh, they ain't going to catch up with us," he said.

He faced forward again. But he got to thinking. There was something strange about the *Bertha Mae*. It was charging along, all right, but the crew was *sitting*. He could have sworn he hadn't seen any poles in the water.

He spun around again. This time he saw the rope, stretching all the way from the *Gullywhumper*'s anchor reel to the *Bertha Mae*.

"Why, you dirty little, low-down. . . ."

As Mike raced to the anchor reel, he could hear hoots and catcalls from the *Bertha Mae*. He could feel his blood boil.

Mike was mad, hopping mad. *Nobody* tricked Mike Fink without paying for it.

CHAPTER 8

Over the next few days the boats traveled down the Ohio River. The *Gullywhumper* was now nearly a mile ahead of the *Bertha Mae*.

As the *Gullywhumper* slowly approached a fork in the river, Mike grinned. He had an evil plan to get back at Davy and his crewmates.

Ahead of them, in the left channel of the fork, there was a large sign sticking out of the water:

DANGER!
TAKE OTHER
CHANNEL

"Get to work, boys!" Mike commanded. "Do just what I told you—and make it fast."

Jocko and Moose hopped out of the boat into the shallow water, and waded over to the sign. It took a couple of tries, but finally they yanked it out.

"Move it! Move it!" Mike barked.

Jocko and Moose sloshed over to the other channel, where they planted the sign firmly in the river bottom.

As they high-stepped back to the *Gullywhumper*, they giggled like two big kids.

Mike smiled with satisfaction. "Ha! Wait until they find themselves going down Dead Man's Chute!"

The *Gullywhumper* rocked with its crew's laughter. Then Mike's crew began poling hard, and their boat quickly slipped past the sign and down the right-hand channel.

A few minutes later, the *Bertha Mae* came charging toward the fork. Davy steered the tiller, looking ahead into the early-morning mist.

The door of the cabin swung open and Cobb came out, rubbing his eyes. "Much obliged for relieving me, Davy," he said with a yawn. "How we doing?"

"We're gaining on them," Davy replied. "They're just around the bend."

Cobb squinted, surveying the landscape. "Mm-hm," he said. "So's the falls."

"Falls?" Davy repeated.

"That's what they call them. Actually it's a stretch of bad rapids down one of the channels. Used to be real dangerous, until they put in the channel marker."

Davy let Cobb take over the tiller. They both watched the fork appear through the mist. The warning sign stood slightly lopsided in the right channel. Cobb smoothly navigated the *Bertha Mae* to the left.

As they entered the left channel, Cobb scratched his head and said "That's funny. I could have sworn the sign was in the other channel on my last trip."

The mist was beginning to lift, but Davy couldn't spot the *Gullywhumper*. All he could see were rocks along the bank, willow trees, a farm in the distance. . . .

And white-water rapids.

The *Bertha Mae*'s crew poled for another few minutes, until the water started tossing the boat around. The men began to stumble. Hank lost his balance and fell on the deck.

"Hey, Cap, it's getting rough," Davy said. "You sure we're in the right channel?"

Cobb's eyes were practically popping out of his head. "Jumping Jehosophats! We're in Dead Man's Chute— someone must have moved the sign!"

"And I think I know who," Davy said, grimly.

Suddenly the right side of the boat lifted clear out of the water. Cobb was thrown to the railing. He clutched the tiller to keep from falling.

Crrrackkkk! came a sound from the hold.

"What was that?" Georgie yelled.

"The timbers are breaking!" Cobb said. "Davy, I'm going to go below and batten down the hatches. You take over."

Cobb opened the cabin door and went down the stairs. Davy took over the tiller, gritting his teeth. He knew Mike had gotten them into this trouble—real trouble—and he was determined to get out of it.

But there was no going back. Not when the current was this strong. Not when the *Bertha Mae* was bouncing so. With every wave, the boat was lifted high into the air and came back down with a loud *slap!*

"Hey, Davy, look out!" Georgie shouted from the starboard side. "There's a rock dead ahead!"

Whack!

It was too late. The *Bertha Mae* had smacked into the rock. The whole crew tossed and tumbled. Davy caught a glimpse of Georgie as he fell to the deck. His eyes were wide, his mouth gaping. At that moment Georgie looked exactly the way Davy felt.

Terrified.

CHAPTER 9

Davy hung on to the tiller. He jammed it to the right as far as it would go. But the boat now had a course of its own. It pitched left and right, following the violent current.

Georgie and Ben struggled to their feet. They pushed their poles against the rocks, desperately trying to avoid collisions.

"We ain't going to make it!" Leif screamed.

"Keep poling!" Davy called back.

A huge spray of water hit Davy square in the face. His feet went out from under him. He tried to grab the tiller, but it was no use. With a loud *shhiisshhh*, he slid across the deck.

The tiller whacked back and forth like an open gate in the wind. Georgie lunged for it, but lost his balance. There was no one in control now.

Cobb stuck his head out of the cabin. "What the devil—?"

The *Bertha Mae*'s bow jolted suddenly upward, sending Cobb tumbling down the stairs.

Then, when the boat hit the water again, it stayed there, bobbing gently, almost completely still.

Georgie opened his eyes. He grabbed the railing and looked over the side. Davy stood up and ran to the tiller. Captain Cobb made his way back up the stairs again and peered out the door.

They could barely believe their eyes. The water was calm again. The narrow channel was flowing back into the Ohio River.

"We made it!" Georgie blurted.

"Yeeee-*haaah*!" Davy cried out in triumph.

"I got news for you," Captain Cobb said, looking behind them. "If you *really* want something to cheer about, take a gander."

Davy turned around. "Well, gol-darn," he said. "I guess Mike knew he was sending us through some nasty rapids—but he didn't reckon he'd found us a short-cut!"

The crew burst out cheering, then picked up their poles. The race was back on.

After their adventure on the rapids, the whole crew was filled with new energy. But below deck, water was seeping in through cracks in the hull. Davy and Ben ran downstairs to help Cobb pump out water while Georgie stayed above to supervise the polers and steer.

For the next few hours, winning the race was not the first thing on everyone's mind. Staying afloat was.

By the time Davy and Cobb finally climbed back up to the deck, night had fallen. The outline of the riverbank was dimly visible in the moonlight. The only sound was the steady splashing of the poles.

Georgie came running up. "Hey, Davy, we're still leading," he said, his eyes shining with excitement. "We might just win this race!"

"Now, Georgie, don't go skinning the bear till we shoot him," Davy replied.

As Davy went to the tiller, Georgie noticed a cluster of lights a mile or so downriver. "Hey, Cap!" Georgie shouted, "what's them lights up ahead?"

"Shawneetown," Cobb replied. "And we've got to put in."

"Put in?" Georgie looked shocked. "And let them hyenas get ahead of us again?"

"Can't be helped," Cobb said. "Everything below is soaking wet, even our gunpowder. And them Indians might jump us any time now."

Georgie knew Captain Cobb was right. Deadly Indian attacks on riverboats had been reported at Shawneetown. Without ammunition, the *Bertha Mae* would be easy pickings.

Georgie sighed and looked away. The *Gullywhumper* was sure to pull ahead now.

As the *Gullywhumper* passed by Shawneetown moments later, Jocko stared at the riverbank. He couldn't see much in the dark, but he could hear Davy's and Cobb's voices.

He ran back to the tiller. "Hey, Mike, listen!" he said. "Sounds like they're putting ashore!"

"Uh-huh," Mike said calmly. "So are we."

"*What?* Are you crazy? Now's our chance to get way ahead!"

Mike smiled at Jocko. "What's the sense of busting our backs when there's an easier way?" he said. He stood up and gestured toward the tiller. "Here, take over."

He walked away, leaving Jocko totally confused.

At the dock the crew of the *Bertha Mae* was working hard. While Davy and Cobb went into town, it was the crew's job to repair poles and patch up the battered hull.

Ben and Hank were at the stern, wrapping thick strips of fabric around their poles. Hank looked back toward the town. "It's pretty late," he said. "Sure hope Davy finds something open."

"Yeah," Ben agreed. "If they don't take too long getting supplies, maybe we can get started again before that Mike Fink shows up."

Hank scanned the river, looking for the *Gullywhumper*. "Ain't no sign of them yet. Hope they don't sneak by us in the dark."

"*Creeeeak!*"

Ben jumped. "What's that?" he asked.

"Just an old bullfrog," Hank said, with a laugh. "If

that ain't just like a city feller—don't even know a bull-frog when he hears one!"

"*Creeeak!*"

Red-faced, Ben got back to work. "Little old rascal's getting pretty close ain't he?" he said.

"Ah, the whole riverbank's full of them," Hank replied.

"*Creeeeak! Creeeeak!*"

Ben had been right about the "little old rascal" getting close. He just didn't realize which rascal it was.

He didn't know that crafty Mike Fink could make his voice sound like a bullfrog. And he couldn't see Mike below them in the dark, loosening the bolts on the *Bertha Mae*'s rudder.

CHAPTER 10

Just beyond Shawneetown, twelve men kept their eyes on the river. Each wore Shawnee clothing. Each had his hair in the Shawnee style and his face painted with Shawnee war paint.

But they were *not* Shawnee Indians. They were river pirates, hired to waylay passing ships. Their clothes were stolen, and so were the wigs on their heads. Only one man could have masterminded a trick like this. Only one man was cruel enough and crooked enough.

Big Foot Mason.

When Mason ransacked a town or looted a ship, no one knew what hit. He struck fast, and he always covered his tracks. His men were masters of disguise, and it didn't matter who took the blame.

The pirates crouched in the bushes and behind rocks, waiting silently.

When the *Gullywhumper* came into sight, one of them whispered, "Get ready."

The men came out from their hiding places. Staying low to the ground, they padded softly toward the riverbank. Soundlessly they lifted off the branches and grasses that camouflaged their canoes.

As the men pushed off into the water, Mason watched. Beside him were his henchmen, the ruthless Harpe brothers, Little Harpe and Big Harpe.

"Ain't you getting mighty ambitious, Mason, taking on Mike Fink and his crew?" Big Harpe said.

Mason sneered. "Ah, we'll take them as easy as we did the others."

He focused his steel-gray eyes on the canoes that were now closing in on the *Gullywhumper*. Laughing softly, he said, "Tonight, my friends, we are going to knock the King of the River off his throne."

At that moment, the *Bertha Mae* was gaining on the *Gullywhumper*. The two boats were close enough for Davy and Georgie to hear Mike shout, "Indians! Let's give 'em what for!"

On the *Bertha Mae*, Davy could hardly believe his eyes. He had always known the Shawnees to be a peaceful, friendly tribe. They would never ambush a keelboat.

"Dad-gum, those *aren't* Shawnees!" he said under his breath.

The *Gullywhumper* was under attack, and Davy didn't stand around when others were in trouble. He picked up his rifle from beside the cabin.

"Tarnation, Davy, they's after Mike Fink, not us!" Georgie protested. "Can't we let him try bragging his way out of this one?"

Davy gave him a look, and Georgie reluctantly picked up his rifle.

The canoes surrounded the *Gullywhumper*. With a mighty heave, Moose tossed a barrel over the side.

It smashed into a canoe and four of Mason's "Indians" dove for safety.

Then two of Mike's men jumped into the water after them. Another two were pulled in by more of Mason's men.

In seconds, the dark, calm water was alive with splashes and grunts and yelps and thuds.

"How can you tell who's who?" Georgie shouted.

"I can't!" Davy shouted back. "Why do you think I haven't shot yet?"

A gunshot rang out from one of the canoes. Jocko jumped as a bullet whizzed past his ear. Wasting no time, Mike reached for his musket. He cocked it, raised it to his shoulder, and fired, smashing a canoe to bits. *Its* men dove into the water.

Mike turned to reload. But just below him, two of Mason's men had him in their gunsights. They cocked their guns, and Mike turned at the sound. He froze. There was no way he'd get his musket up in time.

Crrack!

Davy shot a hole in the bottom of the canoe and the men tumbled into the river.

Crrrack! Crrrack! One shot from Davy, one from Georgie. The Indian imposters were taken by surprise. They sloshed back to shore, much noisier—and much faster—than when they had come. Davy and Georgie put down their guns, but Mike's men had finally gotten theirs. They kept shooting—until the attackers were far off into the woods.

When the sound of the last gunshot faded, Davy called out, "Anybody get hurt, Mike?"

"Nobody on this boat," Mike answered. Then he cast his eyes downward and cleared his throat. As he turned away, he mumbled something else.

Davy wasn't sure, but he thought he heard the word "thanks."

"Hey!" came Cobb's voice. *"Hey!"*

Davy spun around just in time to see Cobb go flying over the side of the boat. In his right hand was the tiller, which had come right off the rudder!

As Davy and Georgie jumped in to rescue their captain, the *Gullywhumper* pulled ahead.

Mike stood on the deck, looking at the *Bertha Mae*. His trick had worked exactly as he had planned.

But Mike wasn't happy. Sure, he wanted to win more than anything, but Davy Crockett had saved his life. When the *Gullywhumper* was in trouble, Davy had jumped in to help.

And what was Davy's reward for his good deed? A sinking *Bertha Mae*, courtesy of Mike himself.

For the first time ever, Big Mike Fink, King of the River, felt ashamed.

CHAPTER 11

"**O**kay, boys," Captain Cobb said, "this here's the town of New Madrid. See if you can guide her into that cove."

The *Bertha Mae* had just traveled south past Illinois, to the point where the Ohio became the Mississippi. The Mississippi was a wide river, with channels and tributaries all along its length. Without a rudder, the *Bertha Mae* was hard to control. The crew had to use their poles to move the boat *and* steer. Everyone was helping out, pushing the boat to the right-hand bank, where they could see a small town through the trees.

Slowly the *Bertha Mae* zigzagged its way to shore. There were three other boats in the cove.

One of them was the *Gullywhumper*.

"Well, will you look at that!" Georgie said. "Guess who decided to take a rest."

As the boat reached an empty spot on the dock, Davy jumped out to tie it fast. "Ben, you and the boys keep watch. Georgie, you go find out where Mike's men are. Cap and I will get the supplies we need to fix the rudder."

"Okay, Davy!" Georgie answered.

"Aye-aye, sir!" Ben said. "Okay, men, all hands on deck—and this time, let me know if you hear any bull-frogs!"

Twenty minutes later, Davy and Cobb were back at the *Bertha Mae*, hard at work fixing the rudder.

It didn't take long for Georgie to return either. "Hey, Cap! Davy!" he called out. "They's coming back!"

"Did they see you?" Captain Cobb asked.

Georgie shook his head. "Nope."

Cobb quickly finished tightening a couple of screws on the tiller. He turned it to the left, then turned it to the right, and said, "Last one to New Orleans is a pole-cat."

They all hopped into the boat. Davy untied the rope and the polers pushed off.

When Mike and his men got to the dock, they all spotted the *Bertha Mae* floating away. In an instant Mike lost every last feeling of guilt.

"Let's get 'em, you lazy swamp rats!" he yelled to his crew.

They all hopped aboard and began to pole furiously. Before long, the race was neck and neck again. No one docked anywhere, no one played tricks. The weather grew warmer each day.

By the time they sailed into the state of Louisiana, the river had become much wider. There were small islands here and there.

Sometimes it was hard to spot the *Gullywhumper*, but Davy had it in his sight at all times.

It was at least a half-mile behind!

Georgie walked up beside him and smiled. "How much longer to New Orleans?" he asked.

"Less than a day, I figure," Davy replied.

"Land sakes, we're going to beat them!" Georgie said. He reared back his head and crowed, "Yeee-*hahh*, we're going to win!"

"Hey!"

A tiny, distant voice made them both turn around.

"Who was that?" Georgie asked.

"Hey! Hey, somebody!" the voice called again.

"Look," Davy said, pointing to an island in the middle of the river.

The island was bigger than most of the others. It was a thick clump of trees and a beachfront, where, waving frantically at them, was a thin, bearded old man. "Somebody get me!" he cried. "I need some help!"

"Hey, Cap!" Davy called over his shoulder. "Swing to that island!"

Cobb pulled the tiller to the right. The *Bertha Mae* veered toward the island. The old man smiled and waded toward them.

"Thank the Lord you stopped," he said, as the *Ber-*

tha Mae came near. His face was wrinkled with age and peeling from too much sun, but he looked happy enough to dance. "Name's Jasper Crowe. You're the first souls I've seen since my flatboat went to pieces and marooned me here. I'm near starved to death."

Davy smiled and reached out his arm. "We can fix that," he said. "Come on aboard."

"Thank you kindly, son," Jasper said. "Mind waiting till I fetch my livestock?"

Cobb's face went pale. "*Livestock?*"

The old man disappeared behind the trees. Seconds later a mule ran out. Jasper followed close behind, holding a chicken in his hands. "Whoa!" he called out to the mule. "Whoa!"

Behind him, a goat and a pig wandered out of the trees.

"Hey!" Cobb said. "We ain't got time to load all them animals. Here comes the *Gullywhumper!*"

They all looked left. Sure enough, Mike's boat was charging along. In minutes it would pass the *Bertha Mae*.

"Cap's right," Georgie said.

Davy shook his head. "We can't just leave them here."

"Well, even if we do get them aboard, we ain't going to have room left to pole!" Georgie insisted. He turned to the old man and said, "Forget about them, Grandpa, and get aboard. We're in a hurry."

Jasper's shoulders slumped. "I can't leave my stock," he said.

" 'Tain't right that he should," Davy agreed. "Come on, boys, let's give him a hand."

Davy jumped off, splashing into the shallow water. Georgie followed him, then Cobb, Ben, and the rest of the crew.

Seeing the men, the mule began racing away. Jasper handed the chicken to Ben and ran after it, shouting, "Come back here, you rascal!"

The chicken began clucking wildly and flapping its wings. "What am I supposed to do with this thing?" Ben shouted, juggling it from hand to hand.

Leif ran by him, chasing a goat. Hank dove after a piglet, which wriggled out of his hands. Davy and Georgie tackled the mother pig, pushing and wrestling her toward the boat.

From the river came a chorus of whoops and yells. "Ain't that obliging of you cornhuskers, just waiting here for us like this!" Mike bellowed from the deck of the *Gullywhumper*.

The mother pig dug her hooves into Georgie's chest and sprang away. Davy grabbed her hind legs and rolled with her on the ground.

"Hey, Crockett!" Mike yelled. "What are you doing? Recruiting a new crew? Haw! Haw! Haw!"

Mike and his men were slapping their knees and clutching their stomachs, weak with laughter.

"This ain't no laughing matter," Cobb muttered. He propped a ramp on the side of the *Bertha Mae* and went back to help the others.

As the *Gullywhumper* floated into the distance, Jasper led the mule onto the ramp.

Davy and Georgie lifted the mother pig over the railing. One by one, the men managed to get all the animals onto the boat.

"Let's go, boys," Cobb said wearily. "It's going to be a long evening."

CHAPTER 12

Three hours later the *Bertha Mae* floated to the mouth of a narrow channel off the Mississippi. Jasper Crowe was the only person smiling.

"That's my place yonder on the bayou," Jasper said, pointing to a ramshackle farmhouse in the distance. "I sure am much obliged for all the trouble I put you to. Got time to break bread with us?"

"We'd like to," Davy said, "but we've got some time to make up."

The old man nodded. "Well, if you're ever back in these parts, my house is always open to you. Now, I'll just get my critters off and let you go on your way."

Ben and some of the other men began helping him unload the animals. Georgie just sighed and shook his head. "I sure got to hand it to you, Davy," he said. "You just don't know when you're whipped."

"Oh, I know we're whipped, all right," Davy said.

Georgie gave him a confused look. "Then why are we breaking our backs to get to New Orleans?"

Davy answered, his voice filled with sadness, "We got to deliver some furs to Mike Fink."

Georgie felt his heart sink. He'd never heard Davy Crockett admit defeat before.

"Well, thank you kindly, Cap," Jasper said. He reached up to the deck of the *Bertha Mae* to shake Captain Cobb's hand. "They's all accounted for, all in the pen. I don't like to think what would've happened if you fellers hadn't saved me."

"Our pleasure," Cobb said. He was smiling, but sadness showed in his eyes, too.

"Good luck!" Davy called out. He knew that stopping to help the old man had cost them the race, but he was still convinced he had done the right thing. Around him, the men picked up their poles and began pushing off.

Jasper looked confused as the *Bertha Mae* began heading back toward the main channel. "Say, fellers," he called out, "I thought you said you wanted to make time."

Georgie was poling as hard as could. He gave the old man an annoyed glance and grunted, "Can't go any faster than this!"

"You could, if you kept going down this here bayou!" Jasper replied.

"What?" Davy said. Instantly the entire crew stopped poling.

Jasper glanced up the narrow channel of water that cut through his property. "If you wanted, you could save forty miles by taking this route."

Davy and Georgie gave each other a look. They couldn't believe what they were hearing.

"I been down it in my skiff plenty of times," Jasper continued. "Runs back into the Mississippi just above New Orleans."

"Looks awful narrow," Davy said. "Think we got a chance of getting through?"

"Well . . . ," Jasper said, looking down the waterway. He stroked his beard, thinking. "It'd be a tight squeeze, but if you'd cut a few trees out of the way and don't mind scraping her bottom a little, you might make it."

Davy could feel his blood starting to pound. Beside him, Georgie looked as if he would explode with excitement. "Georgie," Davy said, "maybe we ain't lost this race yet."

CHAPTER 13

"**S**ome river path," Georgie grumbled, knee-deep in the water. Branches whacked him in the head as he walked ahead of the *Bertha Mae* in the dark of the night. "It's more like a swamp."

In the boat's cabin, Captain Cobb had kept a box of thick machete knives. He'd never used them before—but now they were coming in handy. Georgie was swinging one back and forth, cutting away branches as he waded.

"Hey, Georgie!" Davy called from behind him. "Come back here for a minute. I need you to help me push."

The *Bertha Mae* was stuck in the mud. Four of the other crew members jumped off the deck. Together with Davy and Georgie, they managed to get the boat into deeper water.

Around them, swamp birds swooped and picked fish out of the water. There was also the constant buzz of mosquitoes.

Suddenly, out of the corner of his eye, Davy spotted something slow and slithering in the water. "Watch out!" he shouted.

Georgie whirled around just in time to see an alligator opening its mouth. Its razor-sharp teeth glinted in the moonlight.

"Yeeaaaaghh!" Georgie cried out. He swung his machete wildly. It splashed into the water just to the right of the alligator.

Davy grabbed a pole and smacked it into the water, to the left of the alligator. Its mouth slammed shut and it slithered backward and out of the water.

Georgie mopped his forehead. "That was a close one," was all he said.

By the time the *Bertha Mae* emerged from the bayou, Davy was drenched with sweat. He felt mosquito bites throbbing on his hands and face.

The rest of the crew was exhausted. Ben and Hank could barely lift their poles. Georgie grimaced with pain as he wrapped a bandage around his hand. "Look at this—I have blisters on every single finger!" he complained.

"Hang on, Georgie," Davy said. "We're almost to the Mississippi. It'll be a lot easier there."

Davy was right. As they left the bayou and entered the big river, the powerful current pulled them along.

A tired cheer went up from the crew. Ben and Hank

put down their poles. It was time to relax, time to cele-
brate. The race was the last thing on anyone's mind.

That is, until the *Gullywhumper* pulled into sight.

There it was, poling merrily along the Mississippi—
behind them! Mike and his men were standing at the
bow, their mouths open in shock.

"I don't believe it," Georgie said. "The old codger
was right!"

"All right, we've been practicing long enough,"
Davy announced. "Now let's show them something!"

"Start poling!" Cobb shouted.

Ben and Hank grabbed their poles as if they'd been
resting all day. They plunged them into the water. The
Bertha Mae sped forward.

On the *Gullywhumper*, Mike was shouting himself
hoarse. "Down on them poles, you dirty river rats! If
you don't get me to that landing before Crockett, so help
me, I'll cut every one of you into catfish bait!"

It was a race again. The *Gullywhumper* cut through
the water, matching the *Bertha Mae* inch for inch.

Before long, the lights of New Orleans shone in the
distance. Cobb looked over his shoulder. "Push, boys!"
he commanded. "We're beating them! Push like you
never pushed before!"

The *Bertha Mae* picked up speed, but the *Gullywhumper* was closing in.

Mike eyed the rival boat with a wild glare.

"Moose!" he shouted. "Give them the old one-two punch!"

Moose climbed on top of the *Gullywhumper*'s cabin, carrying his pole. He waited until the *Bertha Mae* was inches away. When Davy's head was within reach, he swung.

Whooooosh!

Davy saw Moose's shadow in the nick of time. He ducked out of the way. The pole swung past him and clipped Hank square in the stomach.

With a yelp of surprise, Hank flew backward into the water.

"Hoooooo-haw-haw-haw!" Mike held his belly with one hand, the tiller with the other.

"So you want to play rough, eh?" Davy said. He grabbed a pole and vaulted himself high in the air. Swinging his legs around, he gave Moose a well-placed kick.

"Yiiiii!" Moose cried, tumbling into the Mississippi.

At that, Cobb burst into laughter.

Suddenly Jocko lunged at Davy with his pole. "Haaaah!" he screamed.

The two of them fenced from one end of the deck to the other, using their poles like swords.

Soon both crews were brawling. Poles sliced through the air, fists flew. Men fell overboard left and right.

"Hit them! Hit them hard!" Mike shouted.

Cobb looked ahead. The New Orleans port was just off to the right. He yanked the tiller, and the *Bertha Mae* cut sharply toward the dock.

So did the *Gullywhumper*.

Now the two boats were neck and neck again. Crewmen scrambled to get back on board. They picked up their poles and ran to the railing.

"Pole, you baboons!" Mike yelled. He jumped from the tiller and grabbed a pole himself. Frantically he thrust it into the water.

It sank into the soft river bottom. Mike pushed as hard as he could, then pulled back up—or tried to.

The pole was stuck, and Mike didn't let go. With a shriek of surprise, he tumbled head over heels into the Mississippi.

"Captain overboard!" Jocko shouted. The crew of the *Gullywhumper* stopped poling to help Mike.

"*Go!*" Davy shouted.

With a burst of speed, the *Bertha Mae* charged into the dock!

"Yeeeeee-*haaaaaah*!" Georgie cheered. Pandemonium broke loose on the deck of the *Bertha Mae*. Davy hugged Georgie, Ben slapped Hank on the back, Cobb danced a jig.

In the water, several yards away, Mike Fink's head bobbed to the surface.

"Hey, you!" Georgie shouted. "You thought you was

going to win our pelts! You thought I was going to pay you for that dinner! Guess you was wrong!"

Sputtering, Mike swam to the *Bertha Mae*. Georgie reached down and helped him aboard.

Mike climbed on deck. The *Gullywhumper* pulled into the dock, its crew shocked and dejected. Looking from Davy to Georgie, Mike shook his head and sighed. "What's the world going to say? Mike Fink, King of the River, losing to a pack of landlubbers."

"I don't reckon we won anything but our furs," Davy said. "That's all we started out to do."

Mike narrowed his eyes in disbelief. "You mean you ain't going to lay claim to my red feather? You ain't going to claim the right to be called King of the River?"

Davy shook his head. "Naw, I'm a lot happier in the woods. I'm not out to be a river man." Then, with a smile, he said, "I reckon there's only one King of the River, Mike."

Mike looked at Davy, his eyes dark with suspicion. But even Mike Fink knew that Davy Crockett was a man of his word. "Where's my hat?" he asked.

"I'll get it," Captain Cobb said. He picked a pole off the deck, stuck it in the water, and fished out Mike's hat.

Mike grabbed the hat off the end of the pole. He looked right and left, scowling.

Then, without wasting another moment, he put it to his mouth and took a bite.

The entire dock rang out with a cheer that could be heard throughout New Orleans. Davy clapped his arm around Mike's back. Mike stared back at him for a moment, then hooted with laughter. Both crews burst into song, rocking back and forth—except Mike, whose mouth was full.

As a crowd gathered around, Davy smiled happily. The *Bertha Mae* had won the race, Captain Cobb had gotten to his destination, and Georgie Russel had gotten out of a load of trouble.

And as for Davy? Well, he'd had his adventure, all right, and now he could sell his furs just as he had planned. But Davy also got something he hadn't bargained for. In Big Mike Fink, King of the River, he had found himself a new friend.

EPILOG

Davy Crockett is perhaps the most famous folk hero of the American frontier. He was born in 1786 and grew up in the rugged country of eastern Tennessee, where his father ran a small country inn. Business was never very good, and the family often relied on young Davy's hunting skills to put food on the table. But even in tough times, Davy had a knack for amusing himself and others with tall tales, a skill that was to later become part of the Crockett legend.

In 1806, Davy married Polly Finley, and they began to raise a family. As the frontier grew more crowded with settlers, Davy and Polly kept moving their family farther west. In 1813, Davy and his family moved for the last time, deep into western Tennessee.

Davy championed the rights of Native Americans in an era marked by great injustice toward Indian people. In 1813, he joined the army in an effort to negotiate an end to the Creek War. His efforts were successful, and in the process he earned the respect of both sides.

Davy returned from the war a hero and was so popular that

he was eventually elected to the United States Congress, where he served three terms. During that time, he helped draft a treaty that would have enabled the Indian people to keep their land. But in 1835, when Congress decided to break the treaty, and his efforts to save it failed, he decided not to run for reelection.

In 1836, Davy Crockett, along with his trusted companion Georgie Russel, joined a small band of brave American settlers under siege at the Alamo in San Antonio, Texas, which was then part of Mexico. The settlers fought long and valiantly in the name of freedom to defend themselves against the Mexican Army, but in the end their numbers were no match for the huge force amassed against them. The enemy soldiers finally overran the Alamo, killing every man, woman, and child within its walls. Davy Crockett died as he had lived—an American hero. And the phrase "Remember the Alamo!" lived on to inspire and unite the Americans in Texas, who eventually won their freedom from Mexico and brought Texas into the United States.